THE POTLUCK

By Elizabeth List
and Yukika Kato

ISBN: 515162818
ISBN 13: 9781515162810

Some days little Tessa needs extra cheer
So she calls her friends from far and near.

"I am hosting a **POTLUCK**,
and I want you there.

Bring your favorite dish,
one that we can all share!"

potluck

[pot-luhk, -luhk]

Also called potluck supper, potluck dinner, pot-luck lunch. A meal, especially for a large group, to which participants bring various foods to be shared.

Tessa sets the table with a smile on her face,

And picks bright yellow
daisies to put in a vase.

DING-
DONG!

Someone is at the door...

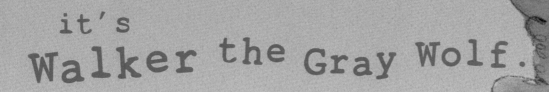

it's
Walker the Gray Wolf.

Tessa has known him forever.
He's a strong, loyal friend,
And he's also quite clever!

Walker's home is the United States
and he brought apple crisp.

DING DONG...

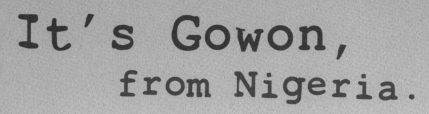

It's Gowon,
from Nigeria.

He is nurturing and wise.
There is strength in his hands,
And peace in his eyes.

Gowon is a
cross-river gorilla
and he made
shuku shuku.

DING
DONG . . .

Here comes Pang the Red Panda!
She's standing tall and proud.

Pang is hoping

will please the whole crowd.

Pang's home is China and she made delicious dumplings!

DING DONG...

another guest is at the door.

Lazaro, the Spanish Lynx,
is guest number four!

Lazaro has brought
gazpacho
all
the
way
from Spain.

Wadley always greets Tessa
with a cheerful
"G'Day!"
He brings his favorite lamingtons
on a bright purple tray.

Wadley is a
hairy-nosed wombat.
He lives in Australia.

Teresa has travelled a long way
from Brazil,
She's holding her pitcher tightly,
to make sure it doesn't spill!

Teresa is a golden lion tamarin.
She made Brazilian lemonade.

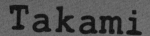
Takami
the Loggerhead Turtle
is our seventh guest,

He traveled from Japan,
so his flippers need a rest!

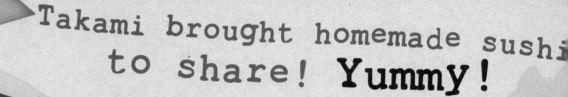
Takami brought homemade sushi
to share! **Yummy!**

10

Ding Dong.

Tessa opens the door.
and lets out a squeal.
Edha has arrived
so they can start the meal!

Edha is an Asian Elephant from India.
she brought palak paratha.

Her friends are all here, the night
feels complete.
Tessa lights a candle as they all take a
seat.

Please let the world know how
wonderful my friends are.

As her friends tell stories and share each dish, Tessa closes her eyes to make a very special wish....

The world is an amazing place because they are in it.

⇶ Recipe for Apple-Crisp ⇶

Ingredients:

3 medium baking apples, cored, sliced thin
1 teaspoon cinnamon
1 Tablespoon sugar
1 Tablespoon flour

Topping:

1 cup quick oats
1 teaspoon vanilla
1/2 teaspoon cinnamon
1/4 cup brown sugar
2 Tablespoons butter or margarine

Directions:

1. Preheat the oven to 325 degrees Fahrenheit (163 degrees Celcius).
2. Mix first four ingredients and place into 9-inch (square or round) baking dish.
3. In a small bowl, mix topping ingredients until crumbly. Sprinkle toppings over apples.
4. Bake for 30 minutes, or until apples are soft and topping is golden brown.

Recipe for Shuku Shuku

Ingredients:
1 cup unsweetened flaked coconut
1/4 cup superfine sugar
3 egg yolks
1/2 cup self-rising flour

Directions:
1. Preheat oven to 350 degrees Fahrenheit (175 degrees Celcius).
2. In a medium bowl, mix together the coconut, sugar and egg yolks to form a stiff dough. Squeeze into 1 inch balls, and roll each ball in flour to coat. Place on a baking sheet, spacing about 2 inches apart.
3. Bake for 20 minutes in the preheated oven, or until golden.

Recipe for Dumplings

Ingredients:

1 2/3 cup coleslaw mix (chopped cabbage and maybe carrots)
1/2 cup chopped bean sprouts
4 scallions, chopped
2 Tablespoon low-sodium soy sauce
1 Tablespoon sesame oil
1/2 Tablespoon grated fresh ginger
15 round dumpling wraps

Directions:

1. In a medium bowl, stir together the coleslaw mix, chopped bean sprouts, scallions, soy sauce, sesame oil and ginger.

2. Heat a 10-inch skillet over medium. Once its hot, add the contents of the medium bowl. Cover the pan and cook for 2 minutes. Uncover, stir and let cook for an additional 2-3 minutes until most of the liquid is evaporated. Remove from heat.

3. Working with one dumpling wrapper at a time, spoon about 1 teaspoon of filling into the center. Moisten the edges of the dumpling wrapper with water (use your finger to spread it around). Then, fold the wrapper over, sealing the edges together with your fingers. Place on a foil-lined plate. Repeat until all of the dumplings are filled and sealed.

4. Heat 1-inch of water in a large pot fitted with a steamer insert. Once it's boiling, spray the insert with cooking oil spray and carefully add the dumplings to the pan. Only add enough to form a single layer, without the dumplings touching. Cover and steam for 5-7 minutes, until cooked through. Serve immediately.

Recipe for Gazpacho

Ingredients:
2 (14.5 ounce) cans diced tomatoes (I use Hunt's Petite Diced)
1/2 cup water
2 Tablespoon extra-virgin olive oil
1 seedless cucumber, cut into 1/4-inch dice
1 small yellow bell pepper, seeded and cut into 1/4-inch dice
1 small onion, cut into 1/4-inch dice
2 medium garlic cloves, minced
2 Tablespoons lime juice
Salt and freshly ground black pepper

Directions:
1. Process 1/2 cup of tomatoes, along with the water and oil, in a blender or food processor until pureed.
2. Transfer to a medium bowl, along with remaining ingredients. Season with salt and pepper to taste.
3. Refrigerate until ready to serve (can be made several hours before serving).

Recipe for Lamingtons

Ingredients:
1 cup butter
1 cup sugar
4 eggs (beaten)
2 cups of self rising flour

Icing:
2 cups powdered sugar
1/3 cup cocoa
½ ounce butter
½ cup milk
shredded coconut

Directions:
1. Preheat oven to 350 degrees Fahrenheit (175 degrees Celcius).
2. Grease a 13 x 9 inch pan and set aside.
3. Cream together butter and sugar. Gradually add the eggs, mixing well.
4. Add 1/3 cup of flour at a time, stirring gently after each addition. Pour batter in pan and bake for 55 minutes. After 30 minutes, reduce the temperature to 325 degrees Fahrenheit (163 degres Celcius).
5. Let cool. Cut into 2 inch squares.

Icing:
1. Melt the butter in a saucepan and remove from the heat.
2. Sift the powdered sugar and cocoa into the saucepan. Then add the milk and mix through.
3. Dip squares of into the icing mix. Roll in coconut, and you're done!

⇛ Recipe for Brazilian Lemonade ⇚

Ingredients:
2 large limes
½ cup of sugar
3 Tablespoon sweetened condensed milk
3 cups water
ice
+ a blender
+ a strainer

Directions:
1. Wash limes thoroughly. Cut off the ends and slice into eight wedges. Place limes in a blender with the sugar, sweetened condensed milk, water and ice.
2. Blend in an electric blender, pulsing 5 times. Strain through a fine mesh strainer to remove rinds.
3. Serve over ice. If you like, garnish with extra lime wedges!

Recipe for Sushi

Ingredients:
2 cups short-grain or medium-grain sticky rice
1 package seaweed sheets (nori)
2 whole carrots
1 cucumber
1 avocado
cream cheese (block form)
soy sauce (for dipping)
 + a bamboo sushi roller

Directions:
1. Cook rice according to package.
2. Clean and peel the carrots and cucumber.
3. Slice carrots and cucumber lengthwise to create long, narrow strips.
4. Remove avocado from skin, remove pit, and slice narrow strips lenthwise.
5. Slice cream cheese into long, narrow strips.
6. Place a seaweed sheet on sushi roller and spread sticky rice evenly across the sheet, leaving a one-inch strip of seaweed exposed.
7. Place a carrot strip, cucumber strip, cream cheese, and avocado across the rice bed.
8. Lightly dab the exposed tab of seaweed sheet with wet fingers (This will act as a "glue" to hold the wrap together).
10. Roll the sushi forward until it makes a complete roll.
11. Cut roll into 1 inch pieces and serve.

Tip: You can put anything you like into your sushi! Mushrooms? Strawberries? Experiment!

⫸ Recipe for Palak Paratha ⫷

Ingredients:
1 cup wheat flour
2-3 Tablespoon olive oil
1 teaspoon Jeera (cumin)
1 cup uncooked spinach
1 teaspoon red chilli powder
1/8 teaspoon turmeric powder
Salt (as needed)
Water (as needed)

Directions:
1. Dump the flour into a large bowl, and set aside.
2. Wash the spinach. Tear off and discard the stems, and chop the leaves roughly. Heat a pan with oil and jeera in it. Add the chopped spinach and fry at low heat.
2. Cook for 2 minutes, then add the spinach to the bowl of flour. Add remaining ingredients, except for the water.
3. First mix the flour well with spinach and then add enough water to make a non-sticky dough.
4. Make 6 equally sized balls and roll them out to look like pancakes.
5. Heat pan, drizzle some more oil and cook the parathas both sides at medium heat, until golden brown spots appear. Serve when cool.

YOU CAN MAKE A DIFFERENCE!

All of the animals in the book are on the endangered species list.

An endangered species is any type of plant or animal that is in danger of disappearing forever.

The main reason that animals and plants become extinct or threatened is because their habitat has been destroyed or changed. Their habitat is the place where they live. It contains all that they need to survive: space, light, water, food, shelter and a place to breed.

Although people are the cause of most of the problems facing endangered wildlife, we can also be part of the solution! Some species that were once on the brink of extinction are now thriving thanks to a helping hand from conservationists.

To learn more about how YOU can help endangered animals, go to:

www.worldwildlife.org

www.bagheera.com

www.kidsdiscover.com

The Gray Wolf, also known as the timber wolf, or western wolf, is a canid native to the wilderness and remote areas of North America, Eurasia, and northern, eastern and western Africa.

The Cross River gorilla was named a new species in 1904. It is the most western and northern form of gorilla, and is restricted to the forested hills and mountains of the Cameroon-Nigeria border region at the headwaters of the Cross River in Nigeria.

The Red Panda is a small arboreal mammal native to the eastern Himalayas and south-western China that has been classified as vulnerable by IUCN as its wild population is estimated at less than 10,000 mature individuals.

Wombats are short legged, muscular marsupials native to Australia and are about 40 inches long with small, stubby tails. They are adaptable and habitat tolerant, and are found in forested, mountainous areas of south-eastern Australia.

"You cannot get through a single day without having an impact on the world around you. What you do makes a difference, and you have to decide what kind of difference you want to make."
–Jane Goodall

The Spanish Lynx is an endangered cat living mainly in the Iberian Peninsula in southwestern Europe. It portrays many of the typical characteristics of lynxes, such as tufted ears, long legs, short tail, and a ruff of fur that resembles a "beard".

The golden lion tamarin lives in Brazil. It gets its name from its bright reddish orange pelage and the extra long hairs around the face and ears which give it a distinctive mane. It is believed that the tamarin gets its hair color from sunlight and carotenoids in its food.

The loggerhead sea turtle is found in the Atlantic, Pacific, and Indian Oceans, as well as the Mediterranean Sea. It spends most of its life in saltwater and estuarine habitats, with females briefly coming ashore to lay eggs.

The Asian elephant lives in Southeast Asia from India in the west to Borneo in the east. It is smaller than the African elephant and has the highest body point on the head. The ears are small with dorsal borders folded laterally.

YOU can make a difference for endangered animals! Talk to your parents, teachers, and friends about creative and effective ways you can make a difference. RESEARCH ONLINE OR AT YOUR LIBRARY. Write them down and commit to them today!

HERE ARE SOME WAYS I WILL HELP SAVE ENDANGERED ANIMALS:

28372640R00018

Made in the USA
San Bernardino, CA
27 December 2015